# NATHAN THE NEEDLE
# AND
# OTHER STORIES
# BY RABBI GITIN

**AS TOLD TO MICHELLE GABRIEL
AND ILLUSTRATED BY BONNIE STONE**

Published in 1994 by Gabriel Press

**Library of Congress Cataloging-in-Publication Data**

Gabriel, Michelle
Nathan The Needle And Other Stories By Rabbi Gitin

Summary: Stories told to children at Temple Emanuel in San Jose, California, during the fifties and sixties by Rabbi Joseph Gitin, as told to Michelle Gabriel and illustrated by Bonnie Stone.

ISBN # 0-9643475-0-4

For information, contact:

Gabriel Press
14510 Big Basin Way #212
Saratoga, CA 95070-6082

# FOREWORD

I would like to express my thanks to my colleague, Rabbi Meyer Heller, for relating to me some of the children's stories used in this book.

I am especially indebted to my dear friend, Michelle Gabriel, who listened to these stories which I had shared with the children of Temple Emanuel, San Jose, California, during the High Holy days when I served as its Rabbi. As a writer and a teacher she has put these oral stories together in written form for future generations to enjoy. As you can appreciate, the enthusiastic participation of the children in the sanctuary at the time these stories were told greatly enhanced the interest in and enjoyment of the stories.

Rabbi Joseph Gitin

# INTRODUCTION

Rabbi Joseph Gitin served as spiritual leader of Temple Emanuel in San Jose, California, for 26 years, from 1950 until 1976 when he became Rabbi Emeritus. During that time his name was synonymous with Judaism, Temple Emanuel, and the entire community at large. He was, on occasion, referred to as the "Messiah" when first introduced as the new Rabbi of this congregation, as "mentor" by other Rabbis and religious school teachers, and as "God" by a young child who, upon receiving a blessing, looked up at him and said "thank you God"—to which Rabbi Gitin replied, "you're welcome!"

Rabbi Gitin not only presided over a congregation of 150 members at the time he started with Temple Emanuel in 1950, he also became a frequent guest speaker at churches, social gatherings and fraternal organizations throughout San Jose. A practice that continued through the early nineties.

"I'm so sold on Judaism that I'm always very anxious to share its pearls of wisdom and profound insights with all people, whether they are Jewish or not," he has stated. "I am primarily a teacher and have always spoken from the vantage point of Judaism."

Rabbi Gitin is known for his warmth, intelligence and quick wit. His down-to-earth wholesomeness endeared him not only to the Jewish community, but to the non-Jewish community as well. His biography includes numerous memberships, board positions, honorary awards, special recognitions and countless accolades that could fill an entire book. Together with his wife Rosalie, the Gitins have spent almost half a century participating in the growth and spiritual direction of San Jose's community of Jews and non-Jews alike.

"Our temple is our spiritual address," he is quoted as saying. "Here we learn that our faith and discipline of Jewish ethical values prepare and equip us to live meaningful lives. Here our children find out who they are and what it means to be Jews."

It was with this philosophy that Rabbi Gitin developed his series of children's stories based on the moral and ethical teachings of Judaism. For the High Holy days, during the fifties and sixties, children gathered in the sanctuary to hear the rabbi tell them a story for the new year. He would bring in a different inanimate object each year around which he would weave his story, inviting the children to participate with their comments and questions. Every child who spoke was heard, every question asked was answered.

*Nathan The Needle and Other Stories By Rabbi Gitin* is a compilation of those stories. While the magic of each story lies in the delivery by the charismatic Rabbi as well as the enthusiastic responses of the children, the essence of what he was trying to do still remains. A firm believer that the spiritual teachings and traditions of Judaism are "caught, not taught," Rabbi Gitin not only lived up to his philosophy by practicing what he preached, he has continued to remain an inspiration to others who also believe "if we don't live by it, they won't learn it."

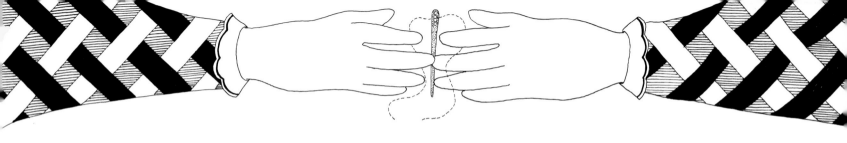

## Nathan The Needle

On one particular Rosh Hashanah morning the Rabbi told the children he was especially pleased to have his good friend "Nathan" with him to help with the service.

The children looked all around the sanctuary and up on the bima but they couldn't figure out who this special friend could be.

Finally the Rabbi reached into his pocket and pulled out a long shiny sewing needle.

"This is my friend, Nathan The Needle," said the Rabbi with a straight face. "And do you know what?" the Rabbi continued. "Nathan The Needle is not just an ordinary sewing needle. Nathan The Needle is like you and me in many ways. So what do you suppose makes Nathan the Needle like us?" asked the Rabbi.

"Well, it has an eye," said a student in the sanctuary.

"Exactly," replied the Rabbi. "You see since Nathan the Needle has just one eye it has to be a good one. Did you know that the Talmud tells us that we too must have a good eye so that we can see the good in others, not the bad. We want to be able to look for good qualities in people and overlook the bad ones. What else is there about Nathan The Needle that's like us?" asked the Rabbi.

"A needle, I mean, Nathan The Needle, can be helpful when it is used to sew a button on a shirt or mend a torn jacket," called out a young girl sitting with her family. "That's what my mother does."

"And Nathan The Needle has a sharp point which can hurt someone's feelings, just like people do sometimes with unkind words," answered a boy in the front row.

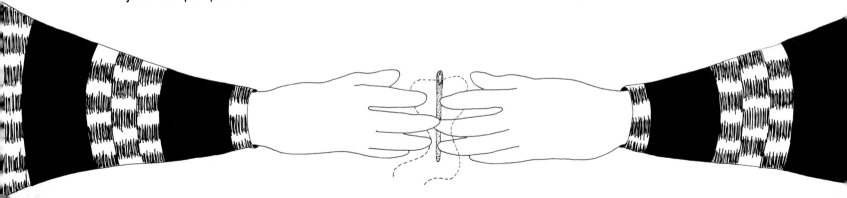

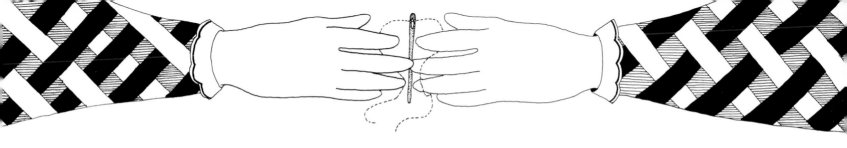

"Those are good examples," responded the Rabbi. "And it is important to remember that just like the sewing needle we too can do things that will either help others or harm them. We help people when we perform acts of kindness and choose good over bad. We hurt people when we tell lies or spread rumors. And sometimes even saying we are sorry is not enough to take away the hurt our words or deeds have caused."

Then the Rabbi told a story from the Talmud. It was about a woman who went to her Rabbi to confess that she had spoken lies about a neighbor and now felt badly that she had done so. She wanted to make amends. Her Rabbi told her to pluck a chicken, scatter the feathers, then gather them up and bring them back to him. The following day she returned and told her Rabbi that she had plucked a chicken and scattered its feathers just like he had told her to do. But when she tried to gather them up again the wind had blown them in all directions. Ah, replied her Rabbi, you see lies are like feathers. Once scattered it is impossible to gather them up again. Nor can the hurt you cause be fully healed. Therefore speak only the truth from now on.

"So my friends," the Rabbi told the children in the sanctuary, "Nathan the Needle wants us to be careful with our words and with our deeds. Nathan The Needle also reminds us to always use our good eye to see the good in others and to choose good over bad so that every action we take is a good one."

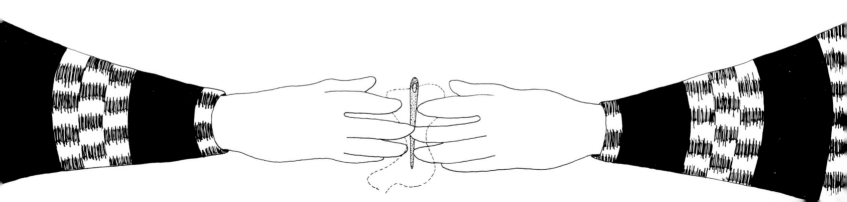

# Peter The Puppet

The Rabbi walked into the sanctuary holding a puppet in his hand.

"This is my friend Peter the Puppet," the Rabbi told the children. "He is here to help me tell you about the wonderful gift God has given to us. The gift of having a mind of our own. But first, can you tell me anything about puppets?"

"Puppets are fun to play with," said one little girl. "And they are fun to watch."

"I like the way puppets can wiggle and jump," answered a boy in the front row. "Puppets can do almost anything someone makes them do."

"Ah," said the Rabbi, "so a puppet can do almost anything someone makes it do. But why not anything it wants to do?" he asked.

"Because a puppet has no mind of its own," replied the children.

The Rabbi smiled.

"That's very true, isn't it? A puppet does not have a mind of its own and can not do anything by itself. Someone has to think for the puppet and someone else has to make the puppet move. So that makes the puppet helpless because it has to depend on others for what it does. But Peter the Puppet reminds us that we are not helpless. We are not puppets because God has given us a mind of our own. What do you think are some of the ways we are able to use our mind?"

"By thinking for ourselves and deciding what is right or wrong," answered a girl in the back row.

"By being responsible for what we say and do," replied the young boy sitting next to her.

"Yes," said the Rabbi. "And we can use our mind to study and to help others. Peter the Puppet also wants us to remember that we have to use our minds to do these things or we will become just like him, a puppet who relies on others for each thought, each sound and each deed."

Then the Rabbi told a story from the Midrash about a Rabbi and a soap maker.

The two were walking together when the soap maker asked the Rabbi just what help religion was in this world. "People are so wicked," he explained. "Just look how they hurt one another, cause war, and destroy property. Religion doesn't seem to be working anymore." The Rabbi, saddened by this comment, said nothing at first. As they continued walking they passed a small child playing in the dirt. "Ah," said the Rabbi. "Look at this child. She is so dirty. What help is all the soap in the world if there is still so much dirt left on the children?" "But Rabbi," the soap maker answered quickly, "don't you realize you have to use the soap in order to be clean, otherwise it doesn't work?" "Aha," said the Rabbi, "so it is with religion. You have to use what our religion teaches in order for it to work."

"You see, boys and girls," continued the Rabbi, "Peter the Puppet can not use his mind to make decisions about what is right or wrong. But we can. Peter the Puppet has to rely on others to think for him and to act for him. But we don't. Because God has given us a mind we are able to think for ourselves. We are able to learn many skills and we are free to choose between good and bad. Now what is important to remember is that we need to use this mind of ours so that we don't become like Peter the Puppet and have others think and act for us."

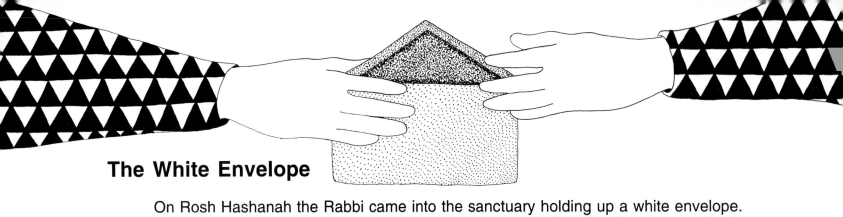

## The White Envelope

On Rosh Hashanah the Rabbi came into the sanctuary holding up a white envelope. "What do you think is in this envelope?" he asked the children. The Rabbi listened patiently as the children called out their answers.

"A letter!" said one, "a Rosh Hashanah card!" said another, and "money!" said a third.

The Rabbi smiled. "Those are all very good guesses but now I will tell you what is in the envelope. It's a mountain!"

The children giggled when they heard what the Rabbi said. They knew it couldn't possibly be a mountain but they also knew that what the Rabbi always told them was the truth. So they waited to see how this could be.

As the Rabbi slowly opened the envelope several grains of sand and gravel fell to the floor.

"These little grains of sand and gravel," the Rabbi explained, "can become a mountain when added to many more grains of sand and gravel. You see, my friends, little things are very important because they can become big things. Can you give me some examples?

"Well an atom is very small but it can power ships to sail over great oceans," an older student in the congregation called out. "And a little gasoline can power the engine of a big car or truck for many miles."

"A tiny seed can become a pretty flower," added his younger sister.

"Bringing money in for tzedakah," said one of the boys sitting in front. "Even if it is a small amount, when it's added to what others bring in it becomes a larger amount."

"My mommy says that when I help her with little chores that helps her a lot," said one little girl softly.

"Saying thank you when someone gives you something," called out a child in the back row. "Or saying yes when someone needs your help and saying no when asked to do something you know is wrong."

"This is wonderful," the Rabbi exclaimed. "You have just told me what we can do to make this new year, this Rosh Hashanah, a better time for others as well as for ourselves. The new year gives us the opportunity to do many little acts of kindness, good deeds and helping others. This adds up over time and makes us feel good because we know we have helped others by our actions."

"And it is important to realize that the opposite is true too. If you tell a little lie it can grow into more lies. When we hurt someone, even a little, that hurt can grow big and hurt others as well."

Then the Rabbi told the children what the Talmud says about the importance of little things. "Don't regard something that is small as insignificant for it can become something great. Be as quick to do a little mitzvah as you would be to do a big one because even one mitzvah, big or small, can lead to others."

"You see," the Rabbi added, "God is present whenever you do a good deed or say a kind word. So every act of goodness you perform, no matter how big or how small, is important. Just like these few grains of sand and gravel can become a mighty mountain, good deeds, when added to more good deeds, can make a very big difference in our lives and in the lives of others."

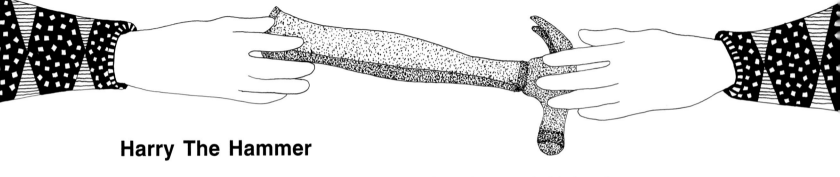

## Harry The Hammer

The Rabbi walked on to the pulpit holding a hammer in his hand.

"This is Harry The Hammer," the Rabbi explained to the children. "Tell me, my friends, what do you see when you look at Harry The Hammer?" he asked.

"I see the head of the hammer attached to a handle," answered one student who thought the Rabbi was joking.

The Rabbi smiled. "That's just what I see too. But you know I also see how very much Harry The Hammer is like us."

The children in the sanctuary laughed when they heard that but the Rabbi assured them that it was so. "I will show you. First tell me which part of Harry The Hammer you think is responsible when it hammers a nail into a piece of wood. Is it the head or is it the handle?"

"The head," called out a few of the children. "The handle," others shouted.

"Both answers are correct," the Rabbi said with a hearty laugh. "While the head of the hammer actually does the hitting, it's the handle that guides the head to the nail. Neither works alone to get the job done, both parts work together. This is true with people as well. You see in our case our handle is our body which, of course, is attached to our head. A person uses his or her head, together with his or her body, to do what needs to be done. Both parts are strong and can be used to build things like schools, hospitals, and homes. Both parts can help or hurt others and both parts remind us to work together to get the job done."

"But how is Harry The Hammer's head and handle like ours?" asked one of the younger students.

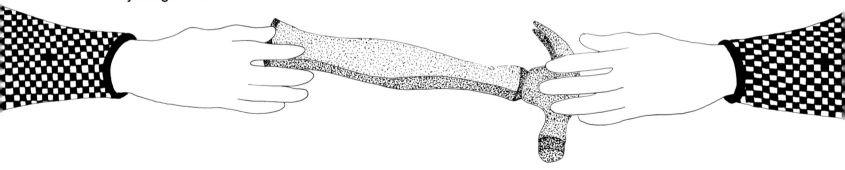

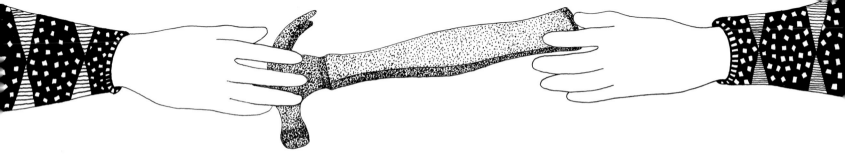

"Well, just like Harry The Hammer uses his head to do the heavy work while the handle guides the head to the nail, we also use our head for the heavy work while our body helps us carry out the job. What heavy work does our head or mind do?"

"Thinking, studying, choosing between right and wrong," answered some of the students.

"Right," agreed the Rabbi. "So just like both the head and the handle of Harry The Hammer are responsible for what it does, we too have to accept responsibility for what we do. We must not look to blame others for mistakes we make."

Then the Rabbi told a story from the Midrash about the man who could not see and the man who could not walk.

The man who could not walk saw some grapes in a farmer's field not too far away. Being hungry he wondered how he could get at it. The man who could not see had the same idea and said: "Stand on my shoulders and guide me to the grapes and then we will both be able to enjoy the grapes." And that was exactly what they did. Later, when they were caught, they each denied responsibility for what they did. "I can't see, so I couldn't possibly do it," said one. "And I can't walk, so I couldn't possibly do it either," said the other. But in fact they were both responsible and both to blame for their actions.

"This story reminds us to accept responsibility for what we do," said the Rabbi. "Blaming others is like saying the head of the hammer works separately from the handle and that one part has nothing to do with the other. And even Harry The Hammer knows better than that."

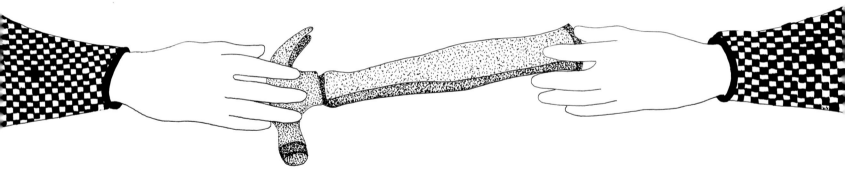

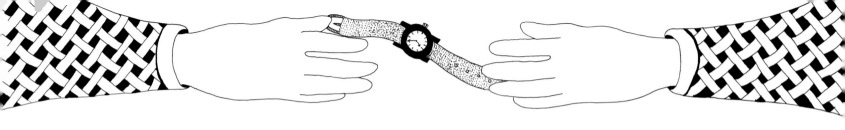

# Wally The Watch

The Rabbi stood on the pulpit for quite a few minutes before speaking. It was time for him to begin his sermon yet he just stood there looking at his watch. The children in the sanctuary began to wonder if the Rabbi was waiting for someone to arrive or if he was late for an appointment.

Finally the Rabbi took off his watch and held it up. "See this watch?" he asked the children. "I call it Wally The Watch because it reminds me so much of you and me."

"Like you and me?" a little girl asked quite surprised to hear that. "Really?"

"Yes," replied the Rabbi smiling. "You see Wally The Watch has two hands and sometimes it runs too fast and sometimes too slow, just like some of us," said the Rabbi with a big hearty laugh.

"But how are the hands of the watch like me?" asked the little girl.

"Well," said the Rabbi, "What do the hands of a watch do?"

"Help us tell the time," called out a student in the sanctuary.

"And what do our hands do?"

"Help us do things," another student called out.

"That's right," the Rabbi answered. "They help us do things, good or bad. So the choice between good or bad is really in our hands. Tell me boys and girls, what do you think Wally The Watch wants to remind us of today?"

"Time," shouted out the children.

"Yes, time," the Rabbi responded. "But what about time? What do you think is so important about time that Wally The Watch needs to remind us?"

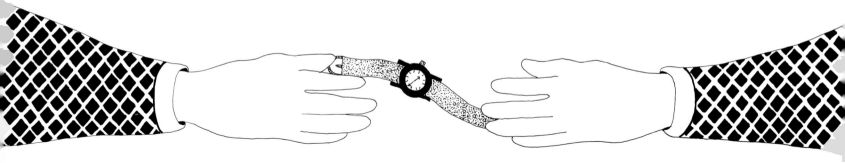

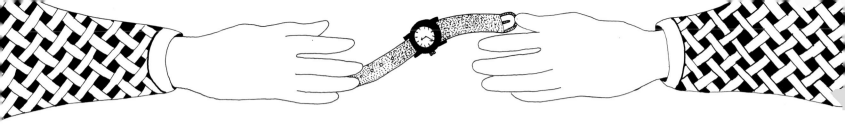

"That we should use our time wisely," answered a boy in the first row.

"What does that mean, to use our time wisely?" asked the Rabbi.

"Not to waste time by choosing to do bad things, but instead using the time to improve ourselves and to help others."

"Okay then," said the Rabbi. How can we use our time wisely and become more responsible for our time?"

"By trying to be on time when we are expected to be somewhere," answered one of the children, "like getting to class on time or home when we're supposed to."

"By taking time to think things through before we do or say something," said another child.

"By taking the time to listen to what others are saying," responded someone else.

"Ah, those are very wise answers," said the Rabbi.

Then the Rabbi pointed out what the Talmud says about the importance of time. "Time is holy and should be used wisely, not wasted," he told the children. "The waste lies in what we can do with time but choose not to—such as when someone needs our help or our understanding and we turn away from them, or when we have the opportunity to study and we don't, and when we rush through our work so quickly we make mistakes and have to do it over again."

"You see," said the Rabbi, "time is a precious gift from God. It goes by fast and is easy to waste. So Wally The Watch would like us to value each minute and to use our time to become the very best we can be."

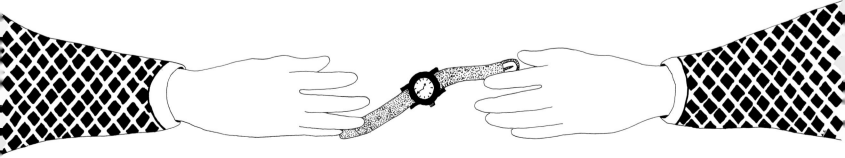

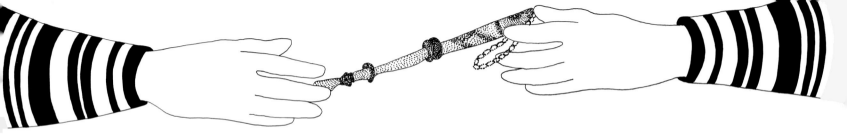

## The Yad

When it was time for the Rabbi to begin his Rosh Hashanah sermon the children were surprised to see him first walk to the Ark and open it. Then he reached in and removed something shiny from around the Torah.

"Do you know what I am going to talk to you about this year?" the Rabbi asked the children.

"The Torah," a few of the children shouted out.

"Choosing good over bad," responded a few others.

"Using the new year to do mitzvot," called out several other children.

"You are all correct, that is exactly what this is all about" said the Rabbi as he held up the beautiful silver Yad. "You see the Yad points to the words in the Torah which is a wonderful resource for stories and lessons for life. Reading stories from the Torah, like the story of Abraham and Isaac, is a very important part of Rosh Hashanah. And choosing good over bad is also an important message for Rosh Hashanah. As we begin a new year we are reminded of the importance of helping others and choosing mitzvot or good deeds to enhance our lives and the lives of those around us."

"Do you know what the word Yad means?" the Rabbi asked the children.

"Yes," the children called out, "it's a Hebrew word meaning hand."

"That's right," the Rabbi said as he held the Yad up for all to see. "And the Yad even looks like a hand. How do you think our hand is like the Yad?"

"The Yad is helpful and good because it is used with the Torah," said a student in the back row. "And our hand can also be helpful when it is doing something good, like helping someone, or patting a friend on the back or shaking hands in friendship.

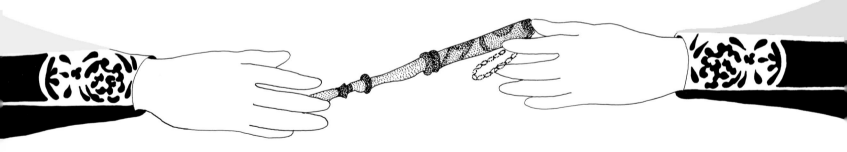

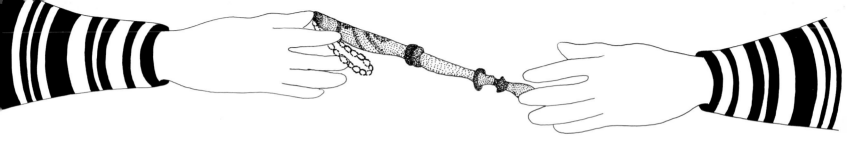

"What are some other ways our hands can be used to do good things?" asked the Rabbi.

"Hands can lift me up when I can't see," said a little girl in the front.

"Hands can come together to cheer when someone does something good, like play the piano or sing a song," said the boy next to her.

"A hand holding on to another hand offers comfort and guidance when someone is frightened or lost," said another small child in the sanctuary.

"And we can also lend a helping hand to others through tzedakah," added the Rabbi. "That's another Hebrew word. Do you know what tzedakah means?"

"Yes," the children responded. "It means helping others so that they are able to help themselves."

Then the Rabbi told the children what the Midrash says about hands reaching out to help others and perform mitzvot. "Abraham had his hands together in prayer. When he interrupted his prayers to God in order do a good deed, God was not angry. God understood that mitzvot, or good deeds, was the best kind of prayer and he was pleased."

"So you see, my friends, Rosh Hashanah reminds us of the importance of doing mitzvot and choosing good over bad. And the Yad, which is used to point out all the good and wonderful teachings found in the Torah, reminds us that doing mitzvot and reaching out to help others is in our hands. As we begin a new year let us choose to use our hands to bring happiness to others through our good deeds. Only we can choose to do the right thing."

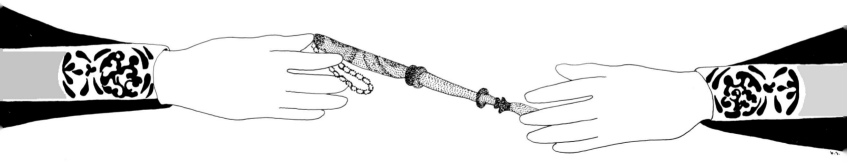

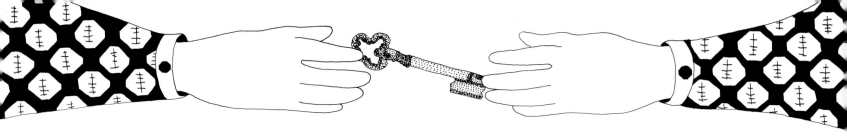

## The Key

The children settled in their seats as the Rabbi walked slowly to the front of the sanctuary. Without saying a word at first, he held up a key for all to see. Then, chuckling a little to himself, he looked around at the children and said he had a riddle for them.

"Why is a key like family, temple and religious school?" he asked.

The children thought about this for a few minutes before calling out their answers.

"Because we wouldn't want to lose any of those things," answered one of the children.

"Because they are all important to us," responded another.

"Because each one opens something," said a student in the back.

"Aha!" said the Rabbi. Those are very good responses. Especially what you said about opening something. Can you tell me what each one opens?"

"Well a key opens doors, locked boxes and diaries," said one girl smiling.

"And our family opens their hearts to us with their love and understanding and help," said a student in the back.

"The temple opens our hearts to prayer and encourages us to give thanks to God for our blessings," added his friend. "And religious school opens our mind to learning more about the history of our people."

The Rabbi smiled as he listened to the responses. "These are wonderful answers," he told them. "You're very smart. You have told me about the importance of keys in unlocking doors and about the importance of these doors once they are opened. You know a key doesn't just open a door it can close and lock it too. So how are we, like a key, able to open or close ourselves to family, temple and religious school?

"We keep ourselves open to the love our family gives us when we respect our parents and obey them," answered an older child. "When we don't listen or don't show respect we are locking them out."

"When we go to temple we open our hearts to the wisdom of Judaism, offering prayers and thanks to God for our many blessings," added his friend.

"And by coming to religious school we keep our minds open to the lessons and teachings of our ancestors, like Abraham, Isaac and Jacob," added another student.

The Rabbi was very pleased with the wise words the children had spoken.

Then the Rabbi told the children the bible story of Abraham. He told them that Abraham lived in a tent with no doors so that he could welcome all strangers who journeyed far across the desert. One day Abraham saw three men walking in the hot sun. He invited them to stop and rest in the shade of a tree near his tent while he brought them "water to wash their feet, bread to eat and cool milk to drink."

"By showing kindness and compassion to others, Abraham was like a key opening up his heart," explained the Rabbi. "When we choose to do mitzvot we not only open our hearts as Abraham did, we are also reminded that God lives through the goodness we show to others. And like a key that opens doors, any act of kindness we do will open our heart and invite God into our life."

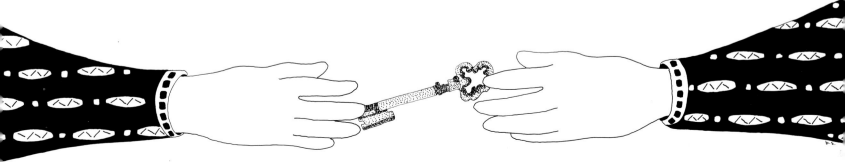

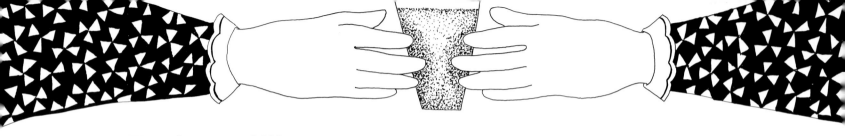

## The Glass of Water

When the Rabbi walked into services carefully holding a glass of water, some of the children thought he had a sore throat or that he had eaten something salty for lunch and was thirsty.

But the Rabbi assured them he was feeling fine and had not eaten anything salty. He had the glass of water in his hand because he was looking for God.

"But isn't God everywhere?" several children called out.

"Of course," answered the Rabbi.

"Then why the glass of water?" the children asked.

The Rabbi just smiled.

"Are you trying to tell us Rabbi that God is in that glass of water?" asked a young boy.

"Yes," said the Rabbi, "and I'm going to tell you how I know that."

Reaching into his pocket the Rabbi took out a sugar cube which he dropped into the glass and mixed with a spoon. Then he asked one of the children to take a sip of the water and tell everyone in the sanctuary how it tasted. When the child answered that it tasted "sweet," the Rabbi pointed out that God is in everything we do that's sweet.

"When you are kind and helpful to others," the Rabbi explained, "that's sweet. When you do your homework and complete your tasks on time, that's sweet. And when you show respect to your parents and teachers, that's sweet. You don't see God when you do something sweet, just like you can not see the sugar that has made this water sweet, but you can sense his presence by the results of your good deeds, just like you can sense the sweetness in the water by tasting it."

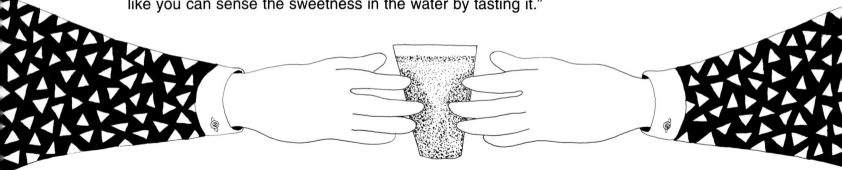

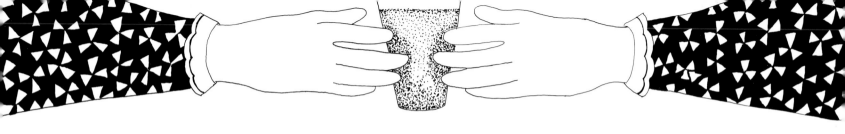

Then the Rabbi told the children a story about a shoemaker who worked hard every day and studied equally as hard every night always hoping that one day he would be able to see God. One night he was awakened by a voice that said: "tomorrow I shall come." He jumped out of bed early the next morning and hurried to the window eagerly waiting for God to arrive. Each time he heard a sound he thought it was God, but there was no sign of him. What he did see was an old man shoveling snow nearly frozen from the cold. The shoemaker brought him in, sat him down near the fire and gave him some tea. When the old man had rested and regained his strength he thanked the shoemaker and left. The shoemaker hurried back to the window to wait for God. Soon he saw a woman with a baby, both dressed in rags freezing from the cold. He brought them in and offered them food and warmth, all the while glancing toward the window for a sign of God. When the woman and child had rested and eaten they too left. The shoemaker continued to help others throughout the day all the while wondering why God had not come. Suddenly it dawned on him. The people he had helped were God's children and by helping them he had made their lives sweet by the goodness shown to them. That is how we see God, he realized, through the good deeds that we do.

"Where is God?" the Rabbi asked. "Wherever and whenever we let him into our hearts. And how do we do that? Like this glass of water which was made sweeter by the sugar we added to it, God is found through the good deeds we add to the lives of others. God is everywhere, my friends, but nowhere unless we add him to our life."

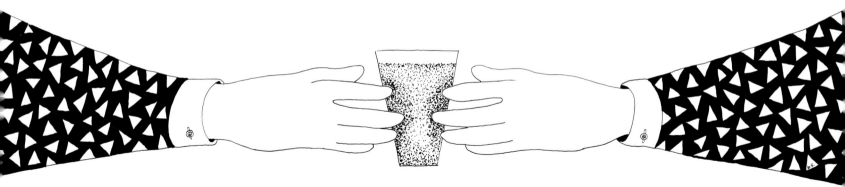

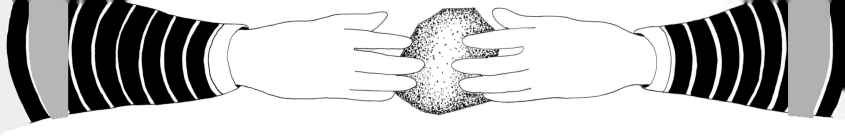

## The Rock

One day the Rabbi brought in a rock. It was an ordinary looking rock so the children were surprised when the Rabbi asked them if they knew that this rock was very much like a person.

The children looked at each other and then back at the Rabbi. They thought and thought about his question for a long while but they just couldn't figure out how a rock was like a person.

"I see you are stomped," said the Rabbi. "So I'll tell you. The reason this rock is like a person is because it is hard, helpful and holy.

"I know a rock is hard," said one little boy, "but how is that like a person?"

"Good question," answered the Rabbi. "And I'm very glad you asked that. You see a rock is hard and sometimes we say that about a person as well. Did you ever hear someone say that someone you know has a heart of stone or is so stubborn and unfeeling we say he or she is hard like a rock?"

The children nodded their understanding so the Rabbi continued.

"But unlike a rock, which cannot change, a person can change. A person, like you and me, can become less hard by being more thoughtful and considerate of others."

"Then how is a rock helpful?" questioned a girl sitting in front.

"That is another good question," answered the Rabbi. "Can anyone give us examples of how a rock can be helpful?"

"Rocks can be used in the building of homes, hospitals and temples," called out a voice from the back row. "And also for roads or for sitting on when you're tired and need to rest."

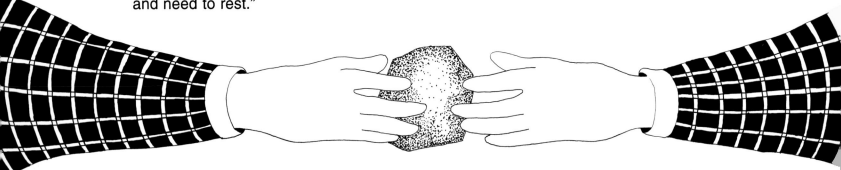

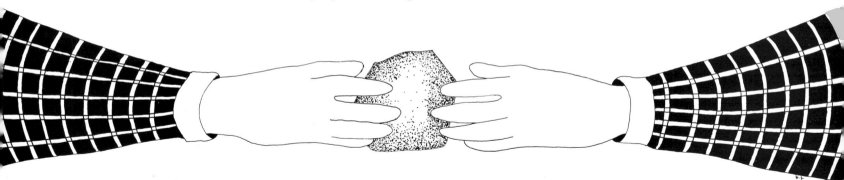

"Right," said the Rabbi. "And how is a person helpful? By being strong and dependable, just like a rock," he explained. "Like when a person keeps a promise and is trustworthy and reliable."

"You also said a rock is holy," asked another child, "what did you mean by that?"

"Well a rock is considered holy because the Ten Commandments were given to us on two tablets of stone which is part of a rock. And in the Hanukkah song, *Rock of Ages*, we refer to God as being our rock and our strength through difficult times. So when a person shows strength during difficult times through compassion, kindness and forgiveness to others, that person is considered holy too. He or she is said to be a rock of the community and a rock of support for his family."

Then the Rabbi told the story from the bible about Rabbi Akiba. One day Rabbi Akiba was watching a little stream running over a large rock. He watched it every afternoon while he rested. It was only a little trickle of water but over a period of many years Rabbi Akiba noticed that the rock eventually split in two from the steady stream of water. If the softness of water could do that to a hard rock, thought Rabbi Akiba, then there was no telling what good deeds a person could accomplish in time if he or she really set his or her mind to it.

"You see my friends," explained the Rabbi, "Rabbi Akiba compared himself to the rock to show how he could set his mind to do anything he wanted to do. We too can compare ourselves to the rock. We can be hard by being dependable, helpful by what we choose to do, and holy by the strength we are to others."

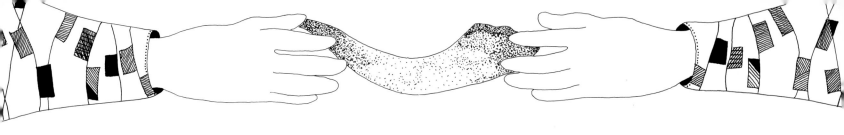

## The Shofar

One year for Rosh Hashanah services the Rabbi walked into the sanctuary holding a shofar. He looked at the children sitting in front of him and then, holding the shofar up high so that everyone could see it, he asked the children to look closely at its shape.

"Doesn't it look a little like a question mark?" he asked. Although it took some imagination to see it quite that way the children agreed that it could in fact resemble a question mark.

"Why do you think that is?" he wondered aloud. "Why do you think the shofar is shaped like a question mark?"

"Because the shape makes it easier to blow?" responded one child.

"Maybe that's just the way it grows on the Ram's head," answered another.

"Hmmm," said the Rabbi, "those are good answers. You know it could also be shaped like a question mark because since it's a Jewish symbol it is meant to encourage us to ask questions Did you know, boys and girls," continued the Rabbi, "that asking questions is an important part of Judaism? Asking questions means we are interested enough to want to know more and motivated enough to want to be involved in the process of learning."

"What questions do we ask at Rosh Hashanah?" called out a voice from the congregation.

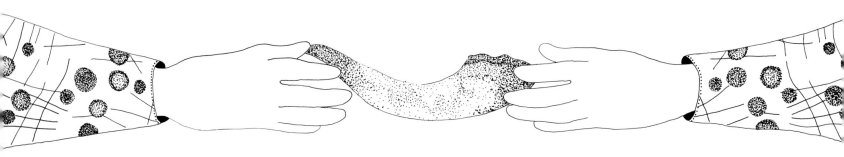

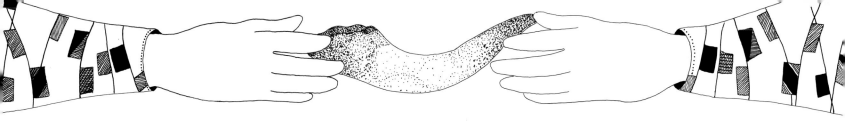

"Good question," the Rabbi responded with a chuckle. "See, you already know the importance of asking questions in order to learn more. So now I'll tell you the answer. For Rosh Hashanah the shofar reminds us to ask ourselves how we can make the new year a better year for everyone. And how does it remind us to ask this question? When we listen to the sounds of the shofar we are able to hear its important message."

*Tekiah*, a short note followed by a longer one, reminds us to ask questions about who needs our help and what we can do to make things better for other people.

*Shevarim*, three rapid notes, is the sound of something breaking. This sound reminds us of the importance of keeping our promises.

*Teruah,* a series of very fast notes followed by the *Tekiah*, is a reminder to do mitzvot, to choose good over bad and to ask what else we can do to help others.

Then the Rabbi told the children a story about Maimonides. He was a great Jewish philosopher who taught that the shofar was a symbol to the Jewish people to wake up and ask questions in order to learn, in order to understand what is going on, and in order to know what God expects of us. The sounds of the shofar tell us to "awaken from our moral slumbers, review our actions of the year and work to improve our ways."

"You see," the Rabbi added," the sound of the shofar is our reminder to follow God's commandments to help others, keep our promises and choose good over bad. At Mount Sinai, when God gave the people the Ten Commandments, the shofar was sounded. And when the people heard the sound of the shofar they asked themselves how they should respond. Then together they answered with the Hebrew phrase—*na-asheh v'nishman*...we will listen and we will do."

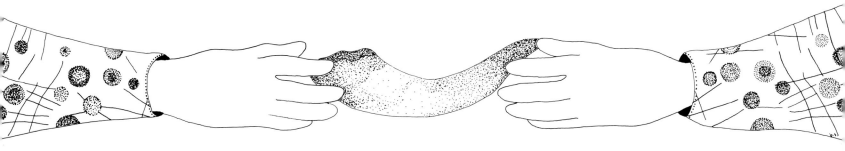

## The Football

The Rabbi came into the sanctuary carrying a football. The children wondered if he was going to play a game with them or tell them a story.

But right away the Rabbi explained that although he was not going to play football with them, not this day anyway, he would appreciate it if they would explain the game to him. The children liked that because many of them knew the game very well.

"Football involves teamwork," said the young boy sitting in front. "Football means working together to get the ball and score a touchdown."

"Yes," added his friend. "It also takes a lot of practice so each player plays his best. And they need to know the rules of the game so the referee doesn't call a penalty when there's a mistake."

"Thank you," answered the Rabbi. "That's very interesting. You know I never realized how much life is like a football game. In football each player has a position to play that's very important to the others on the team and to the results of the game. That's sort of how it is with us. Do you know why what we do is important to those around us and to how we live our life?

"Well we are important to our family, our teachers and our friends," said a girl sitting near the Rabbi. "And our position as a son or daughter, father or mother, teacher or student, makes us part of a team that works together for the best results in life. We also need to help one another and accept responsibility for what we say and do."

"And just like we keep score in football by how many touchdowns are made, in life, we keep score by how we help others and how we strive to reach the goals we've set for ourselves," added another student.

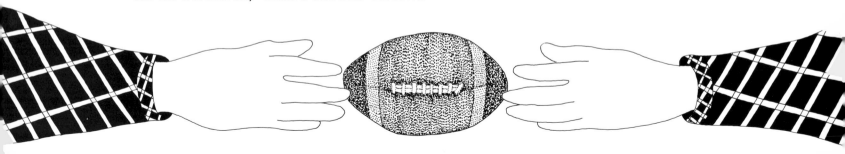

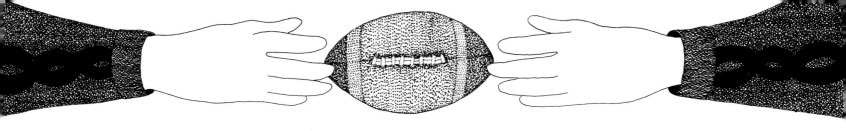

"That's right," said his friend. "Football has a referee to make sure the game is played according to the rules, but we're the referee in our own life. It's our conscience, the small inner voice, that tells us right and wrong. We just need to listen to it."

"Okay, let's see if I have this straight," continued the Rabbi still holding the football in his hand. "Life is like a football game because each of us in life has a role, or position to play. Each person is important to the rest of the team and cooperation is a necessary part of the game plan, same in football, same in life. But wait, if players learn the rules of football from a coach, how do we learn the rules of life?"

"From studying the Torah," shouted the students. "And from our parents and teachers too."

"Isn't this wonderful," said the Rabbi with a twinkle in his eye. "We're all football players in the game of life. Football uses a ball to help players play the game, while in life our mind helps us learn, think, and understand right from wrong. Players rely on a goal post to give them a direction, and we rely on the Torah for our direction."

Then the Rabbi told a story from the Midrash about three men in a small boat. When one man began to drill a hole in the bottom of the boat the others shouted at him to stop. But the man continued drilling the hole insisting that he had paid for his seat on the boat and could therefore do whatever he wanted to do. No, they told him, what you do will result in the boat going down and all of us drowning.

"That story," explained the Rabbi, "reminds us that we are all in the same boat. We are responsible for the well being of others. In life, as in football, we need to work together as a team in order to come out as winners."

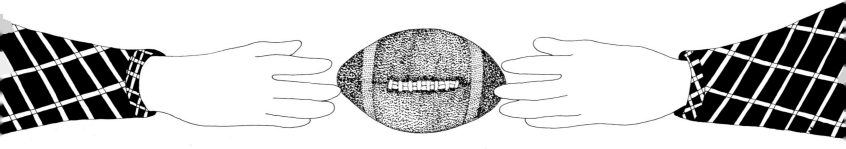

**Michelle Gabriel** is a professional writer with more than 18 years experience writing feature stories and articles for community newspapers and national publications. Her work has appeared in *Young Gideon Magazine* and *Family Circle* magazine. She taught religious school for twenty years at Temple Emanuel in San Jose, California, under the spiritual leadership of Rabbi Gitin and is the author of *Jewish Plays For Jewish Days* a book of plays geared for elementary grade students.

**Bonnie Stone** is a professional artist whose work has been featured throughout the United States. Her Bay Area exhibitions have included "People of the Book" at Chai House in San Jose, "from the right to left" at the Jewish Community Library in San Francisco, "Oy, Butterfly" and "A Decade of Japanese Narrative" at Tandem Computers exhibition space in Cupertino, as well as a series of drawings, "Quilts, Quilters, Quiltings: Narrative Threads of Our Social Fabric" at the American Museum of Quilts and Textiles in San Jose. In addition to receiving numerous awards for her art she has also illustrated *The Yiddish Alphabet Book* published by P'Nye Press (1979) and Adama Books (1988).